"Well, here we are at a party celebrating the publication of the first of the Nancy Drew mystery books!" exclaimed Pam.

"Yes, here we are," said her friend Bess, with a short toss of the head.

"Yes, here we are," echoed Sue, Bess's younger sister, and then, with a challenging look at her two companions, "So now what?"

"Some stairs," said Pam, pointing and then leading the way. "Let's take these stairs."

"Oh, oh, oh," groaned Bess as she slowly followed Pam up the steep marble stairs. "Instead of stairs, I want some refreshments immediately."

"Do I have to come with you?" asked Sue, with a touch of the querulous little sister in her voice.

"I like looking down from the tops of stairs at people who are just milling about," said Pam, ignoring her companions and dashing up the stairs two at a time.

Then, reaching the landing, she turned and looked down on a room filled with people who were in fact milling about and who also held glasses in their hands.

"Refreshments," said Bess, licking her lips thirstily. "I wonder where those people got their refreshments."

"Shall I go all the way down and ask them for you?" asked Sue, with more than a little sarcasm. "And then shall I come all the way back up and give you the information?"

Suddenly, Pam's body tensed.

Her fingers grew taut as she clutched at the balcony rail.

"Look!" she exclaimed in a soft but hoarse whisper.

"Look," she said again, and this time she pointed a finger at something or someone down below.

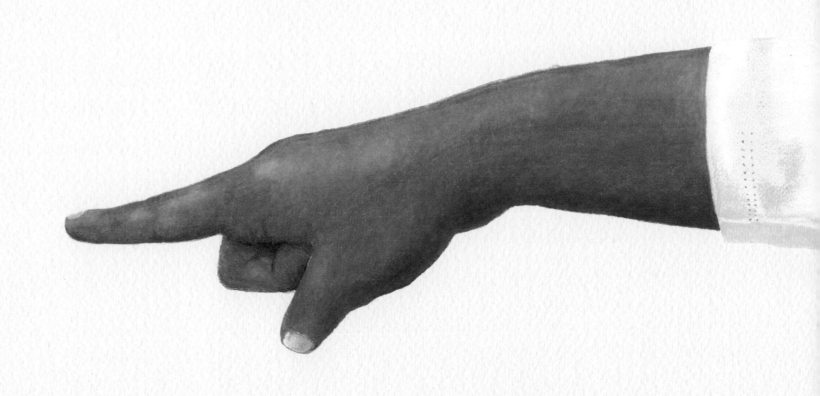

"Oh, oh, oh," said Bess, her eyes growing large and her face turning first a ghostly white, then a vivid red.

"What?" asked Sue, peering at the swirling mass, her head bobbing up and down confusedly.

"But it can't be," said Pam.

"I don't believe it," said Bess.

"What?" asked Sue again, this time with a small stamp of the foot.

"How vile!" said Pam.

"How vile, to say the least!" said Bess.

". . . But . . ." said Sue.

"How bilious!" said Pam.

"How bilious indeed!" said Bess.

"I . . . I . . . I . . . don't know . . . what you are talking about," said Sue, with an almost prehistoric whine in her voice.

"Shall we?" asked Pam, turning to Bess and grabbing her almost roughly by the shoulders.

"Shall we? Shall we?" said Bess, trying to free herself from Pam's now firm grasp.

"Hypers," said Sue. "Shall we what?"

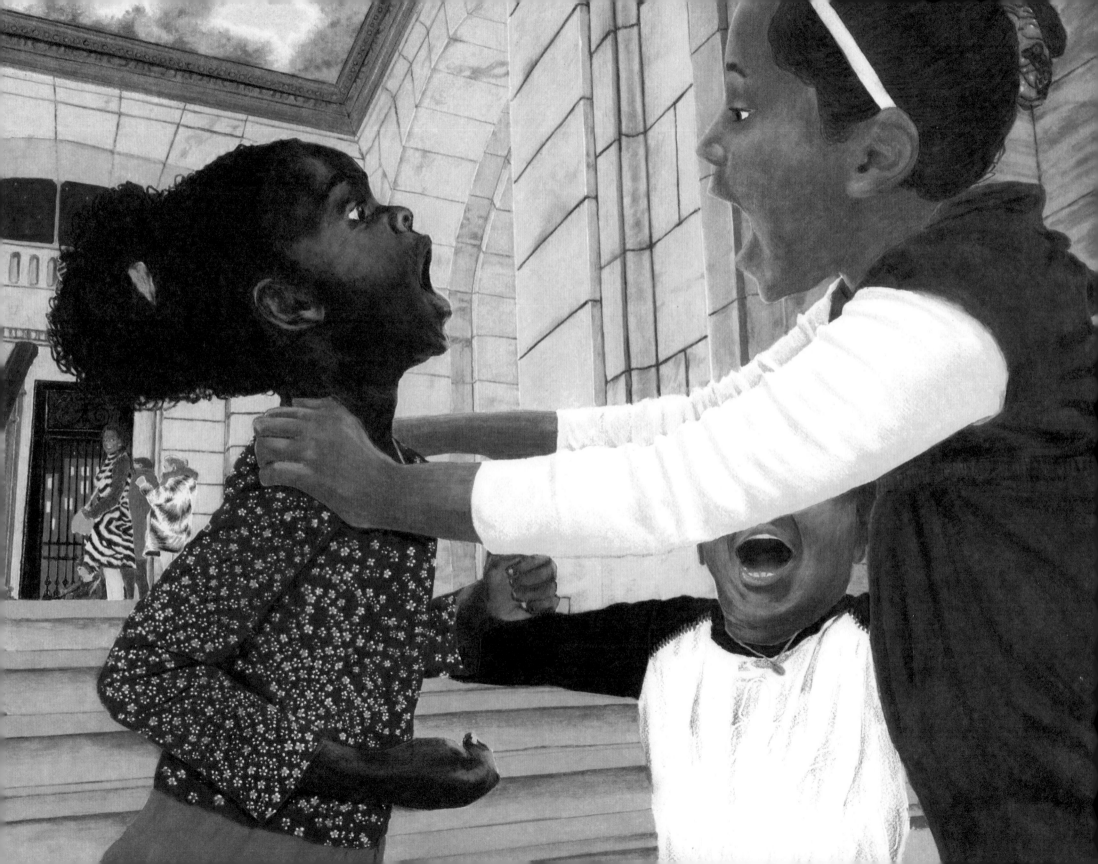

Pam, now locked in indecision, turned back to whatever it was that had caught her attention so firmly before. Her face darkened in puzzlement, her eyes darting here and there furiously and fast.

"It's gone," she said. "Oh dear! It's gone."

"It's gone," said Bess. "It is gone. Oh, oh, oh."

"But what?" said Sue. "And now it's gone. And now I don't suppose you will ever tell me. You never tell me anything."

JAMAICA KINCAID is a writer and professor. Her last novel, *See Now Then*, was published in 2013. The Josephine Olp Weeks Chair and Professor of African and African American Studies in Residence at Harvard University, Kincaid was elected to the American Academy of Arts and Letters in 2004.

RICARDO CORTÉS is the author and illustrator of *Sea Creatures from the Sky*, *It's Just a Plant*, and *A Secret History of Coffee, Coca & Cola*. He is also the illustrator of a #1 *New York Times* best-selling classic for parents about putting their children to bed, as well as the G-rated follow-up, *Seriously, Just Go to Sleep*.

The text of *Party* originally appeared in the *New Yorker* (1980), and was later published in *Talk Stories* by Jamaica Kincaid, ©2001 by Jamaica Kincaid. It is reprinted here by permission of Farrar, Straus and Giroux.

Published by Akashic Books
Words ©2001, 2019 Jamaica Kincaid
Illustrations ©2019 Ricardo Cortés

ISBN: 978-1-61775-716-7
Library of Congress Control Number: 2018960897

First printing

Printed in China
Printing Plant Location: Guangzhou City, China
Production Date: June 2019
Job / Batch #: 83093

Black Sheep/Akashic Books
Brooklyn, New York, USA
Ballydehob, Co. Cork, Ireland
Twitter: @AkashicBooks
Facebook: AkashicBooks
E-mail: info@akashicbooks.com
Website: www.akashicbooks.com

The End